The Adventures of
Owen

ISBN 978-1-63961-588-9 (paperback)
ISBN 978-1-0980-8182-9 (hardcover)
ISBN 978-1-0980-8183-6 (digital)

Christian Faith Publishing, Inc.
832 Park Avenue
Meadville, PA 16335
www.christianfaithpublishing.com

Printed in the United States of America

The Adventures of

Owen

Jo Ann West

Chapter 1

Run, Run

Slurp, slurp.

The tiny calf felt the first warm kisses from his mother.

Slurp, slurp

He could smell her sweet breath.

Slurp, slurp.

He slowly opened his eyes, and his mother stopped to smile down at him.

"Momma," he whispered, and her smile grew bigger.

Suddenly, the young calf was picked up and was carried away from his mother. He could hear her calling after him.

"Moo, moo," she cried. "Moo, moo," and the further away he was carried, the louder her cries became. The young calf called back to her and he tried to wiggle free, but the man carrying him held him tightly.

Plop! Suddenly the calf felt the ground once more beneath his hooves. Then the man that had carried him picked up a metal chain that was attached to a large plastic igloo. He placed the free end of the chain around the young calf's neck.

A second man then appeared and fed the young calf a bottle of milk. The young calf was very hungry, and the milk was warm and delicious. When the bottle was empty, both men walked away, leaving the young calf alone.

Clank, clank. The young calf turned his head to see what was making this noise. Next to him was another young calf who was chained to an igloo as well. As the calf moved, the chain made a clanking noise. Next to him was another young calf chained to another igloo and next to him, another, and next to him, another. There were more calves than the young calf could count!

"Hello," whispered the calf next door.

"Hello," replied the young calf. "Where are we? How long do we have to stay here?"

"Well," answered his neighbor, "we are on a farm, a dairy farm. Our mothers are dairy cows. The men you saw are farmers. They collect our mothers' milk and give it to us in bottles."

"But why? I can collect my own milk!" said the young calf.

"I'm not sure why they do it this way," said the neighbor, "but they do feed us often. Then after about four months, we get to go for a ride on a big truck."

"Where does the truck go?" asked the young calf.

Just then, the chain that had been placed around the young calf's neck fell off.

"Your chain fell off!" exclaimed the calf's neighbor. "You are so lucky."

"His chain fell off!" the young calf heard over and over as the word spread.

"Run, little calf. You're free!" someone yelled.

"Yes, run!" said another.

Suddenly, all the other calves were yelling, "Run, run!"

"Caw, caw!" two black crows sitting in a tree also yelled for the young calf to run.

"Run, run!"

"Caw, caw!"

The young calf ran and ran until his young legs grew weak and could no longer hold him up.

Plop. He collapsed on a bed of fresh spring grass. Exhausted, the young calf fell sound asleep.

Chapter 2

Friends Forever

"Poor kid," commented Santino, one of the black crows that had followed the young calf away from the farm, rooting for him all the way.

"I wish there was something we could do to help him," Kesia replied to her husband. "Do you think he will make it? He is so young!"

"We will hang around for a while and watch over him," Santino reassured his wife as the two crows settled down on a tree branch.

The young calf dreamed of his mother. She was covering his face with warm kisses. "That tickles, Momma," said the young calf. Then suddenly, he was running, being chased, but he didn't know who or what was chasing him. Faster and faster he ran.

"Hola!"

The young calf opened his eyes to see two crows staring at him.

"Hola," the male crow repeated. "I'm Santino and this is my wife, Kesia."

"Hello, uh, I don't know my name," said the young calf, "but it's very nice to meet you."

"Where are you headed?" asked Santino.

"I don't know that either." The young calf frowned.

Suddenly, the three of them heard the hum of a motor, and it was growing louder and louder.

"Sounds like a truck." Santino frowned, thoughtful. "Hide behind that tree, little calf. I will go and see what it is."

Kesia kept the young calf company as her husband flew toward the noise. Santino returned after a few minutes. "It's a truck full of sheep," he told them.

"What are sheep?" asked the young calf.

Just then, a big truck appeared on the road. In the back of the truck were sheep, so many sheep. They bounced up and down with every bump in the road.

"Those poor sheep!" exclaimed Kesia. "Look away, little calf."

"Why, where are they going?" asked the calf.

Just then, the truck went over a *big* bump. Suddenly, one of the sheep went over the side and onto the road.

"Oh no!" cried the calf.

The two crows flew over to the sheep who lay on the road. The calf followed on foot.

The female sheep, called a ewe, opened her eyes slowly to see three pairs of eyes staring at her.

"Hola," said Santino and Kesia.

"Hello," said the little calf.

"Hello," replied the ewe as she tried to stand up.

"You had quite a fall, little lady. Maybe you should lie there for a few minutes before you try to get up," advised Santino.

"No, the truck might come back for me. I must move and hide," explained the ewe.

The ewe stood up and limped off the road as the young calf and the crows followed.

"Are you hurt?" asked the young calf as he noticed a mark on the ewe's side.

Santino and Kesia glanced at each other knowingly as they also looked at the red "54" on the ewe's side.

"No," replied the ewe. "I think I'll be all right."

"Allow me to introduce myself," said the male crow. "I am Santino and this is my wife, Kesia."

"Very pleased to meet you," the ewe replied. "I'm… Haley," she heard herself say, remembering a time long ago when she did have a name.

"I don't have a name," the calf said sadly.

Haley looked up at him. "You have nice eyes," she told the calf. "I once knew a young boy who loved me. He would pick me up and kiss my head. He had nice eyes too. His name was Owen. Would you like to be called Owen?" she asked.

The young calf whispered the name and smiled.

"Owen," repeated the crows.

"I like it," said Santino.

"I like it too," said Kesia.

"Well then, Owen it is!"

The ewe was happy to help.

Suddenly, Haley noticed all of the luscious, spring grass.

"Yum," she exclaimed as she began to chomp on it. After watching her, the young calf took a bite of the grass as well.

"Yum is right!" he exclaimed. They continued to eat side by side until the sun went down. Both were exhausted from the day that each of them had had. They fell fast asleep under the stars as Santino and Kesia kept watch over them.

Owen dreamed of his mother again.

Owen and Haley spent the next morning grazing on the spring grass and then took a nap. After that, they spent the afternoon grazing and once again slept side by side beneath the stars. Santino and Kesia were never far away.

When Owen woke up the next morning, Haley was nowhere to be found.

"Haley," called Owen. "Haley."

No answer.

"Haley," Owen called again.

"Santino, Kesia," Owen called out.

The young calf suddenly realized he was all alone and began to cry.

"Baa, baa," heard Owen. "Baa." He walked toward the sound and there near a tree lay Haley with a baby lamb beside her. Santino and Kesia were there, as well.

The lamb was as white as snow with a pink nose and the cutest ears that stuck out of her head sideways. Owen's heart grew warm, and he smiled.

"Hello, Owen. I'd like you to meet my daughter. I've had many lambs in my lifetime but was not allowed to keep any. This little one will remain with me forever—forever and ever and ever and everly. That's it! Her name is Everly!"

Owen was so moved that he felt a tear drop from his eye.

"Hello, Miss Everly," said Owen. Everly smiled up at Owen as she snuggled close to her mother.

Owen told Haley, Santino, and Kesia how afraid he had been when he woke up and could not find any of them. He asked them all, even little Everly, to form a pact with him that they would always stay together, through thick or thin, no matter what, for the rest of their lives, and they all agreed.

Chapter 3

Home Sweet Home

The following day, Haley and Owen once again spent the morning grazing in the beautiful field of green grass. Dotted throughout the field were hundreds of yellow dandelions, which both Haley and Owen found to be scrumptiously delicious. Miss Everly hopped about between them as she played, stopping every so often for a drink from her mother.

Santino and Kesia had flown off early that morning in search of a tree in which to make their nest. Soon they would have eggs to keep safe. This would be their fifth year of hatching eggs together.

As the morning turned into afternoon, Haley and Owen grew tired for a nap. Miss Everly was already asleep on a thick patch of grass in the shade of a large oak tree. Haley lay down next to her daughter quietly so as not to awaken her. Owen lay down on the other side of Miss Everly.

"Do you think I will ever see my mother again?" he asked Haley.

"Perhaps you will," Haley replied. "Life is full of surprises."

Owen drifted off to sleep as he pondered Haley's answer.

Crack. Boom!

Haley, Owen and Miss Everly were startled awake.

"What was that?" whispered Owen with fear in his eyes. Just then, there was another boom, and they all turned toward the noise. Far off in the distance, they could see dark rolling clouds covering the sky. Suddenly, the clouds lit up with a bright light, and then came the loud boom again.

"It's a thunderstorm," Haley explained, "and it's headed right toward us."

Just then, Santino and Kesia appeared.

"Wow, that's some storm headed our way!" exclaimed Santino. "Kesia and I found the perfect tree for our nest, and we think that you three can also make your home there with us."

Haley was very skeptical. "But we can't climb trees."

"You don't have to," Santino replied. "Just trust us and follow along before the rain starts. We must hurry though. Those clouds are moving fast."

Haley, Owen and Miss Everly followed Santino and Kesia as they flew toward the forest. As they entered, the atmosphere became different. The temperature grew cooler, and the light was dancing off everything it touched, as it was now filtered through the trees. Birds were singing lovely songs, and the leaves rustled as squirrels and chipmunks gathered nuts from the ground. A family of deer were busy eating leaves and berries from a bush, but they stopped to nod hello as the group of newcomers passed.

Suddenly, there standing before them was the tallest, biggest, most amazing pine tree that anyone has ever laid eyes on. The group stopped in awe. Santino and Kesia flew to the bottom branches of the tree, which lay on the forest floor. They each took a branch and flew up, lifting the branches, which created a doorway into a very large hollow at the base of the tree.

"*Nuestra casa es tu casa*. Go in, *mis amigos*, to your new home," Santino and Kesia invited.

Haley, Owen and Miss Everly slowly entered the space. It was dark and cozy, and it smelled so good, like pine. The floor was soft beneath their hooves with many layers of pine needles.

"Look up," Kesia said excitedly. "Here is our nest."

As the three looked up, they could see Santino and Kesia proudly perched on the nest that they had painstakingly built that morning.

"This is perfect!" Owen said delightedly.

"Thank you, Santino and Kesia," Haley said through tears of joy.

"*De nada*. You're welcome, *mis amigos*," replied Santino and Kesia.

Life was good.

As the thunderstorm passed overhead, the group of friends settled into their new home, and not a drop of rain spoiled their joy.

As the day drew to an end, the group of friends told each other stories of the world outside as they knew it. Santino and Kesia were very wise. They had traveled many distances and had learned a lot about the world and the people who lived in it.

Haley shared stories as well of the farms that she once lived on. She spoke fondly of the boy, Owen, who had loved her. She had moved to another farm when she was still young, but she had never forgotten the boy, Owen.

Owen, the young calf, wondered about his mother and the dairy farm where she lived.

Soon the group grew tired and fell fast asleep in their new, safe, and very comfortable home in the Great Pine.

The next morning, they were all awakened by a commotion outside the Great Pine. Owen was the first to explore. There was a group of rabbits running around frantically. When they saw Owen, they asked him if he knew where George was. They explained that a young deer was wounded. He had a twig stuck in his ear and he was in great pain. George was known in the forest as the forest doctor. He had hands that could tend to injuries, whereas many of the other animals did not.

"But who is George?" asked Owen. "Tell me and I'll help you find him."

"He is a very wise and kind groundhog. He lives in tunnels underground, and we cannot find him."

Just then, a large brown groundhog appeared. "Is someone looking for me?"

After listening to the rabbit's story, he followed them to the injured young deer. The deer lay on the ground, moaning in pain. His mother and father stood over him. George got to work as soon as he arrived. He carefully removed the twig and then washed the wound and applied a salve that he made from different plants to prevent the wound from becoming infected. The deer family thanked George and offered him some of their berries, which he declined to take. He bid them farewell and turned his attention to the audience that had gathered. He looked up and became quite amused when he saw a male calf, a female ewe, a lamb and two black crows watching him.

"Hello and welcome to the forest," he said with a warm and sincere voice. After introductions, George led the group to a stream, where he washed his instruments. All of the animals were delighted to see the stream, and they all drank the delicious cold water. George spent the day with the group and told them all about the forest and all the animals that lived there. George had become a friend on that day, a good friend, one that would visit often.

Chapter 4

Christmas

Soon, the fall came and went, and then winter was upon them. The snow was wonderful, but Haley, Owen and Miss Everly had to dig through it every day to find the grass hidden beneath. Their home in the Great Pine was always warm and dry. The stream never became frozen solid, so they always had plenty to drink.

One night, as the group of friends gathered in their home, Haley told them the story of Christmas. She explained that it came from a book that had been read to her by Owen, the boy with the kind eyes whom she once knew.

She told them about the joy of Christmas, which celebrates the birth of Jesus, the son of God, who was born to Mary in Bethlehem in Judea. She told them how Mary and her husband, Joseph, had to travel far right before the birth of Jesus and how a humble donkey had carried Mary so she wouldn't have to walk. Haley told them how none of the people would give Mary and Joseph a room and

how only the animals had welcomed them into their barn. She proudly told them how God had chosen the animals, just like them, to be the only ones to witness the miraculous birth of His son and that animals were the first on earth to meet him.

That night, they all fell asleep with a sense of pride, knowing that they, too, are precious in the eyes of God.

When Christmas morning came, they all celebrated the birth of Christ, and they gave thanks to God for choosing animals, just like them, to welcome Mary and Joseph on that glorious night when the Lord Jesus was born.

Chapter 5

Life Is Full of Surprises

One beautiful spring afternoon, Haley and Owen were in their favorite field grazing on spring grass and dandelions when they noticed Miss Everly had wandered too close to the road. It was the same road where Haley and Owen had met. They both called out to her, but she was too busy eating to notice.

"I better go get her," Haley said as she began to walk toward her daughter. Her gait had slowed down lately. She wasn't as young as she used to be. Owen followed. When they got to where Miss Everly was, they knew why she had ignored them. There, they found her in the middle of a large patch of delicious clover. Yum, Haley and Owen joined Miss Everly. They were so engrossed in eating the clover that they didn't hear the approaching truck. Suddenly, Owen saw it off in the distance but fast approaching.

"Oh no, run!" Owen and Miss Everly ran as fast as they could. but when they got to the edge of the forest, Haley wasn't with them.

"We've got to go back," said Owen, and they both ran back to where they had left Haley. They found her lying on her side.

"Get up, Momma!" cried Miss Everly.

"Hurry!" insisted Owen. "The truck is coming." He nudged Haley with his nose. "Please, Haley, get up," he pleaded.

"I don't think I can," said Haley weakly. "Please, Owen, get Miss Everly to safety. I'll be all right. I'll come in a little while."

"But you can't stay here. That might be the truck that you escaped from. Please, Haley, try," Owen continued to plead with her.

Suddenly, the truck was approaching where Haley lay on the side of the road.

"Go, Owen. Please save my daughter. Go!" instructed Haley.

"We'll go get George. He'll know what to do. Put your head down, Haley, so the truck can't see you." Owen and Miss Everly ran as fast as they could to try to find George.

Haley put her head down. She was so tired. She had been growing old and tired for some time now. Then she heard the truck slow down and come to a stop. She heard the sound of the door open and close, and next, she heard footsteps approaching her. She was too scared and tired to lift her head.

"God, please let Owen and Everly be safe," was her only prayer as she closed her eyes tightly with fear. Then a man knelt down beside her, and he gently touched her head.

"Are you all right, little one?" he quietly asked as he stroked her cheek. The man's voice was kind, and it gave Haley the strength to open her eyes, and when she did, she looked up into the kindest, most familiar eyes that she had ever seen, the same eyes that she knew when she was just a lamb. It was Owen, her Owen who had named her, her Owen who used to hold her and kiss her head. As their eyes met, Owen looked at the freckle pattern on Haley's nose, and he recognized her.

"Haley? Is it really you, Haley?" he asked in amazement.

Haley rubbed the top of her head on Owen's chin, and he knew it was her.

"Oh, Haley, I thought you were… I cried so hard the day my father sold you and put you on that truck. A lot has changed since then. I have converted my father's livestock farm into a sanctuary where all animals live out their lives happy and loved. I'm going to take you there and take good care of you. You will have many friends, I promise. I can't wait to introduce you to my wife, Brianne, and our children, Michael and Kayla."

Just then, Owen the calf came out from behind a tree and began to snort and dig at the ground in a show of aggression in an attempt to frighten the man away from Haley. When the man saw Owen, the calf, acting like the bull he would one day be, he chuckled.

"So you are the group that people have been talking about. Where is the lamb?" Owen the man asked.

He knew of the group through gossip. People had seen a wild cow, a wild sheep, and a wild lamb who were living in the forest. They had been spotted several times by the townspeople.

Haley called to Owen the calf and told him not to be afraid. She told him that the man was the same Owen that he had been named after. She told him to get Miss Everly and that Owen was going to take them to his sanctuary to take care of them. Owen did as she told him.

Once at the sanctuary, Haley was evaluated by the doctor; she was getting old and was also anemic, but he said with the right supplements, she would be fine.

Haley, Owen and Miss Everly had to remain in quarantine for a month before they could meet the other animals, so they spent that month in the barn. During that time, they learned that Owen started the sanctuary after his father had died. Some of the first animals that Owen had taken into his sanctuary came from the dairy farm not too far away. Owen had always felt sorry for the dairy mothers whose babies were taken from them. He often could hear their cries and vowed that one day, he would help them. Shortly thereafter, Owen approached the dairy farmer about taking some of the older female cows who would soon be sent to slaughter. It took a lot of convincing, but the dairy farmer finally agreed to let some of his oldest cows go to the sanctuary. That was several years ago. Now the sanctuary was filled with many different kinds of animals from many different situations. One thing that was constant was the love and attention given to each animal by Owen, Brianne, Michael, and Kayla.

The month passed quickly, and by the time the quarantine was over and the group was ready to meet all the other animals, Haley was stronger, still old and slow on her feet, but she was very happy. Owen and Brianne guided them all out to the grand pasture where Haley, Owen and Miss Everly were delighted to find green grass and dandelions. They were so busy eating that Owen didn't notice the large female cow standing beside him until she started to shower him with kisses. He recognized her smell immediately. "Momma!" It was her. He couldn't believe it! Haley was right. Life is full of surprises.

After that day, Haley, Owen and Miss Everly settled into their new lives. Owen could always be found in the great field next to his mother with Haley and Miss Everly close by. Even Santino and Kesia had made their home at the sancturary, and this is how they lived out the rest of their lives—happy, safe, and loved.

About the Author

Jo Ann West grew up in a large devout family in Providence, Rhode Island. She married at a young age and has raised four wonderful children. She now has six grandchildren. All of the characters in *The Adventures of Owen* are named after her children and grandchildren. She is also a Registered Nurse. She has always loved animals, as her mother before her, and she would like to see change in the way they are treated, especially in the meat and dairy industries. Change is only possible with enlightenment and education, and that is the author's goal in sharing the story of the animals in her book. She is amazed by the selfless heroes who have founded the growing number of animal sanctuaries around the world, like the character Owen and his family. Please support them.

CPSIA information can be obtained
at www.ICGtesting.com
Printed in the USA
LVHW071615300921
699022LV00006BA/52